ALISON WINN

Aunt Isabella's Umbrella

Illustrated by Glenys Ambrus

 CHILDRENS PRESS, CHICAGO

Library of Congress Cataloging in Publication Data

Winn, Alison
  Aunt Isabella's umbrella.

  SUMMARY: Arabella's aunt gets mad at her for not
handling the umbrella properly, but the next time
Aunt Isabella uses it, she has some trouble herself.
  [1. Umbrellas and parasols—Fiction] I. Ambrus,
Glenys. II. Title.
PZ7.W7297Au   [E]   76-50026
ISBN 0-516-03579-7

American edition published 1977 by
Regensteiner Publishing Enterprises, Inc.
All rights reserved. Printed in the U.S.A.
Published simultaneously in Canada.

Text copyright © 1976 Alison Winn
Illustrations copyright © 1976 Hodder & Stoughton Ltd
First published 1976 by Knight books and
Hodder & Stoughton Children's Books, Salisbury Road, Leicester
Printed in Great Britain

U.S. 1962427

Great Aunt Isabella
has got lots of umbrellas.
Lots of umbrellas, and
they all hang up on hooks.

3

One looks torn and rusty,
one looks worn and dusty.

4

One has spots of gold and yellow.
"I like that a lot," said Arabella.
"Look! One end is like a hook.

"If it rains tomorrow,"
said Arabella to her
Great Aunt Isabella,
"May I borrow that umbrella
with a handle like a hook?"

5

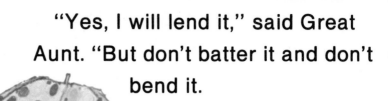

"Yes, I will lend it," said Great Aunt. "But don't batter it and don't bend it.

See! You put it up like this

and you put it down like that."

Next day it rained and rained.

"Good-bye, Arabella," said Aunt
Isabella. "I must trust you to look
after my spotted umbrella."

"I will," said Arabella, and
she put up the umbrella.

7

She set off down the street. Pitter
patter. Her feet went pitter patter.

The jolly lady looked and said, "My,
I like your spotted umbrella!"

Arabella was so proud of that umbrella.

She saw the rain had stopped but
she did not put it down.

The black clouds still looked full of
rain.

At the bus stop Arabella tried to
close the umbrella. She *had* to close
it now to ride inside the bus.

But she could not get it down. She
had to keep it up. It took a lady's hat
off with the end that's like a hook.

An old fellow got wet as he sat on the seat. Drops of rain from the umbrella dripped on his hat and dropped on his feet.

Aunt Isabella had no notion of the fuss and the commotion.

BANG BANG.

The busman rang the bell, and stopped the bus.

Poor Arabella! Just look at that umbrella! She has battered it and shattered it, because it wouldn't close.

She was sorry that she did it. She was sorry so she hid it.

But rain spots pattered on her head and tears ran down her nose.

15

So Arabella took the umbrella out again.
She put it up to stop the wind and rain.

And SWOOSH it took her off her feet,
and SWOOSH blew inside out.

Aunt Isabella was mad at Arabella.
She was mad and sad to see that
battered, shattered, bent umbrella.

"I'll have to send it to a man who can
mend it," she said. "There's a man who
mends umbrellas in a cellar in the
town."

So Aunt Isabella took the battered
umbrella. She took it to the man who
had a shop down in a cellar.

He was big and fat and jolly and said,
"Golly what a mess! Call again
tomorrow. I'll make it look like new."

Next day Aunt Isabella went to town
for her umbrella. It looked like new.
The man said, "I can say without a
doubt that it will *not* blow inside out."

Next day was wet and windy.
Aunt Isabella took her umbrella
when she went out shopping.

It did not turn inside out. But
SWOOSH a sudden gust of wind just
blew her . . .

. . SWOOSH away.